8/04
50

THE ALIENS ARE COMING!

LISA THIESING

DUTTON CHILDREN'S BOOKS ★ *NEW YORK*

For Robin and Susan, the aliens

Library of Congress Cataloging-in-Publication Data
Thiesing, Lisa.
The Aliens are coming! / by Lisa Thiesing.—1st ed.
p. cm.
Summary: Peggy becomes very worried when she hears that the
Aliens are coming.
ISBN: 0-525-47277-0
[1.Miscommunication—Fiction. 2. Musicians—Fiction. 3. Rock
music—Fiction.] I. Title.
PZ7.T35615Aj 2004
[E]—dc22
2003019303

Published in the United States 2004 by Dutton Children's Books,
a division of Penguin Young Readers Group
345 Hudson Street, New York, New York 10014
www.penguin.com
Designed by Jason Henry
Manufactured in China
First Edition
1   3   5   7   9   10   8   6   4   2

It was a lazy day.

Peggy thought that she would

stay inside and listen to the radio.

"What a catchy tune!" Peggy said.

"I like it!"

She snapped her fingers along with the music.

Suddenly, the announcer broke in.

"We interrupt this program for

an important news flash!

The Aliens are coming!

They have taken over Europe!"

"Europe! Oh my!"

Peggy looked at her globe.

"Let's see… Europe is way over there,

and I'm way over here.

Nothing to worry about."

A few days later, at breakfast,

Peggy turned on the radio.

"The Aliens have taken over Japan!"

"The Aliens again? Hmmm," said Peggy.

She got out her atlas and found Japan.

"That is very far away."

A few days after that,

there was a special news flash on TV.

A reporter came on and said,

"The Aliens have invaded our country!

I've never seen anything like it!"

"California!" Peggy squealed.

She looked at her map of

the United States.

"Well, that's on the West Coast.

And I'm in the East. But...

they're getting closer."

Peggy was starting to worry.

The next day,

Peggy began preparing

for the invasion.

She went to the store

to buy some supplies.

When she got home,

she moved all her things

to the middle of the room.

She made a nice, safe bunker.

I'll be fine here, thought Peggy.

She listened to her ham radio.

"Aliens rock Cleveland!"

Ooooh, they're getting closer!

she thought.

The next morning,

there was more bad news.

"Oh, no! They're getting even closer!"

That evening, Peggy turned on the

local news.

"The Aliens are coming to our town!

They will be landing here tomorrow!"

"HERE!?" gasped Peggy.

She spent all night

in her bunker.

In the morning, she crawled out

of her bunker.

"Where are all the little people

from outer space?" Peggy asked.

Later that day, she heard a knock!

"Oh no! The Aliens! They're here!"

Peggy ran for cover.

The knock got louder.

"Hurry!" Peggy heard.

"Let me in! It's me! Kathy!"

Peggy opened the door.

Her friend Kathy was shouting,

"The Aliens are coming!

The Aliens are coming!"

Peggy was so glad to see her.

She pulled Kathy inside.

"Are you all right?" asked Peggy.

"No!" said Kathy.

"I think I'm going to faint!"

"They say the Aliens are landing

at the airport!" said Kathy.

"Look at my map.

See how close they'll be?"

"The airport is there and my house is...

HERE!

That's much too close!"

said Peggy.

"It's getting late.

We've got to go!" said Kathy.

"Right!" said Peggy. "Let's run!"

Peggy could hear sirens wailing.

The Aliens have landed!

The sound was getting louder and louder.

Great mobs were forming on the streets.

Everyone was screaming.

Everyone was fainting.

"This is terrible," thought Peggy out loud.

As evening fell,

the crowd got thicker and thicker.

Everyone was chanting,

"Aliens! Aliens!"

Kathy had to pull Peggy along.

"I can't believe we're going

to see the Aliens!" said Kathy.

"I can't believe it either!" moaned Peggy.

They fought their way to the front.

"Oh, we're so close!"

Kathy was thrilled.

"Oh, we're so close!"

Peggy was scared.

It was a pitch-black night.

All of a sudden,

there were bright, flashing lights

and loud, booming sounds.

Then Peggy heard music.

It was loud. It was booming.

She had heard this music on the radio.

"Look at them! Aren't they great?"

shouted Kathy.

"You mean the Aliens are…

a *band*?!" asked Peggy.

"Of course, silly.

What did you think?"

"Oh, never mind," said Peggy.

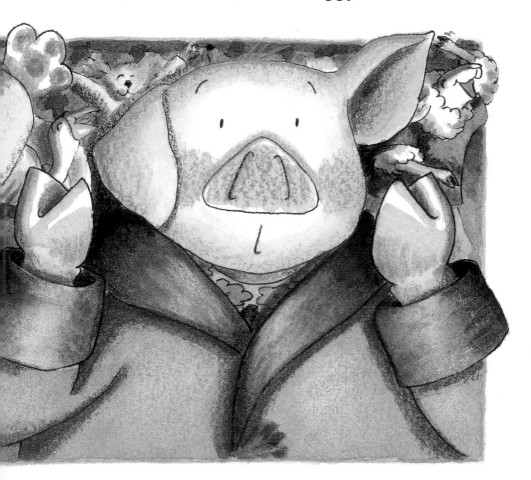

Everyone was dancing!

So they started to dance, too.

"Don't you love them?" asked Kathy.

"The Aliens? Yeah!" said Peggy.

"They're out of this world!"